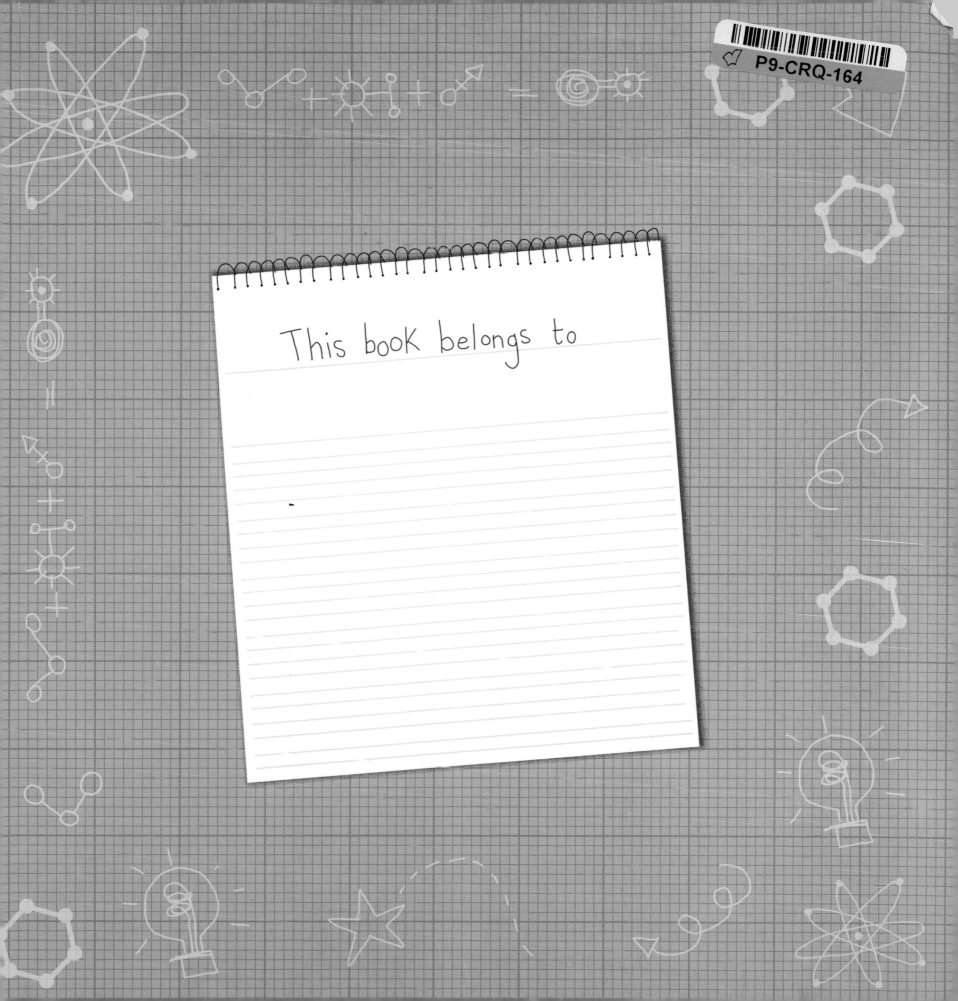

This book belongs to

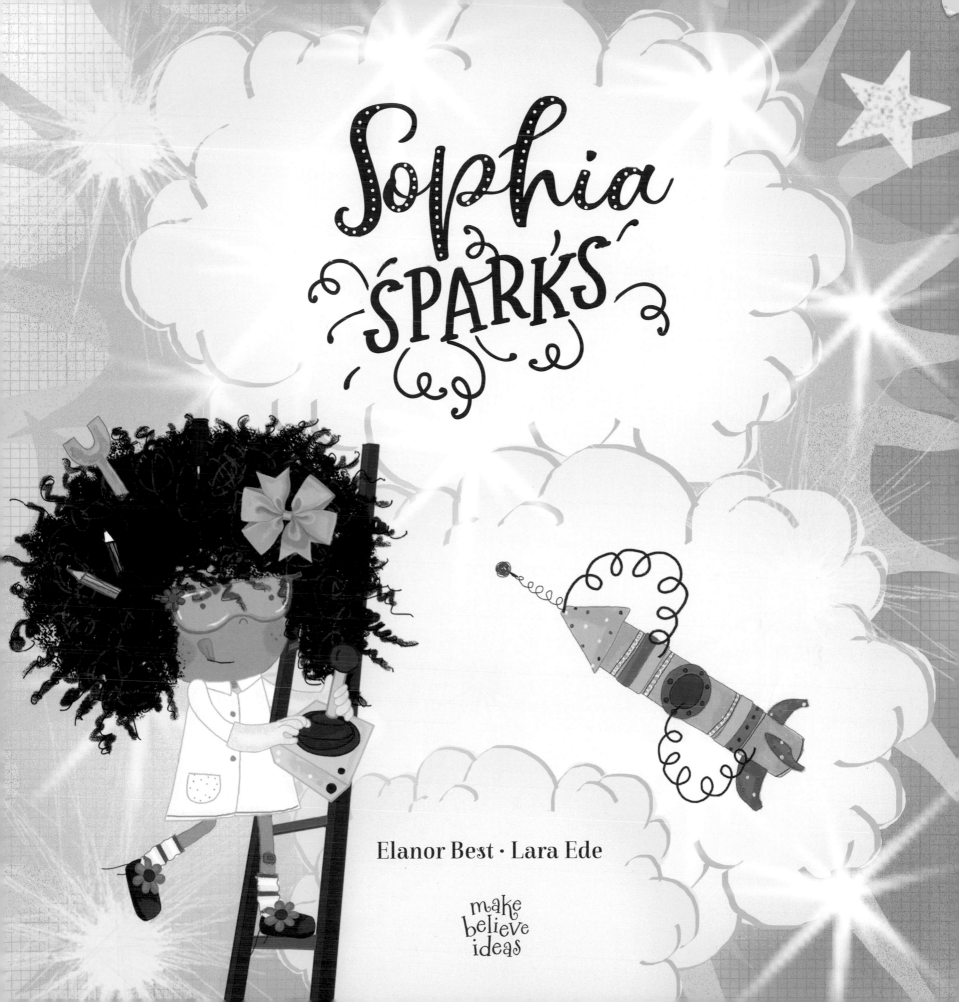

Sophia Sparks

Elanor Best · Lara Ede

make
believe
ideas

A glance at *Sophia*
will draw your **attention**
to the *bow* that unlocks
her flair for **invention**.

This *bow* is the **key**
to her skill, she is **sure**:
when she **wears** it,
she **thinks** of
inventions galore.

With her *bow* on her head,
she can make **ANYTHING!**
From glitter-fueled ROCKETS
with **jet-thruster** springs . . .

to ROBOTS that dance
as they tie up your laces,

and HOUSES with **legs**
that compete in **long races**.

But no one invents **different** things like *Sophia*.
Instead, all her friends work on just **one** idea:

Isaac builds
JET-ENGINES
out of bright steel;

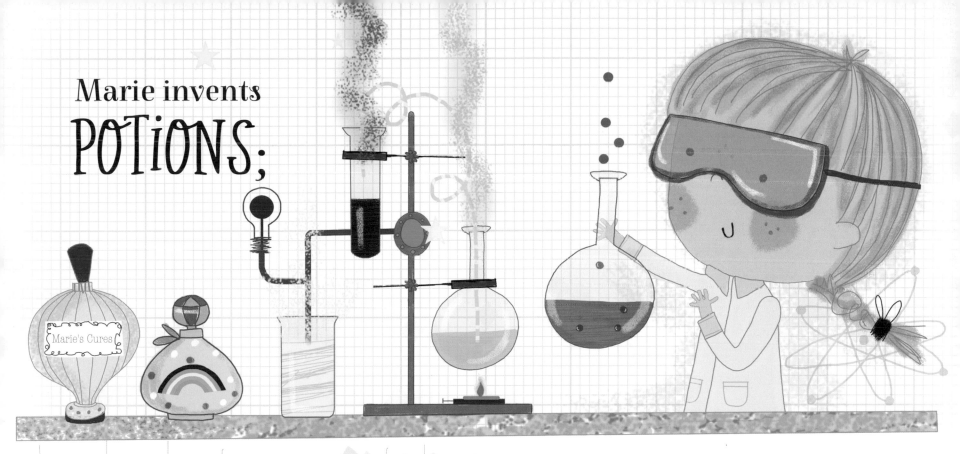

Marie invents POTIONS;

Marie's Cures

and Nick builds NEW WHEELS.

One day, the students
were given a **TEST**:

change sign

to **transform**

their old bus
and make it the **best**.

Sophia reached out
for her trustworthy **bow**,
but saw, with **dismay**,
it had **vanished** –

"OH, NO!"

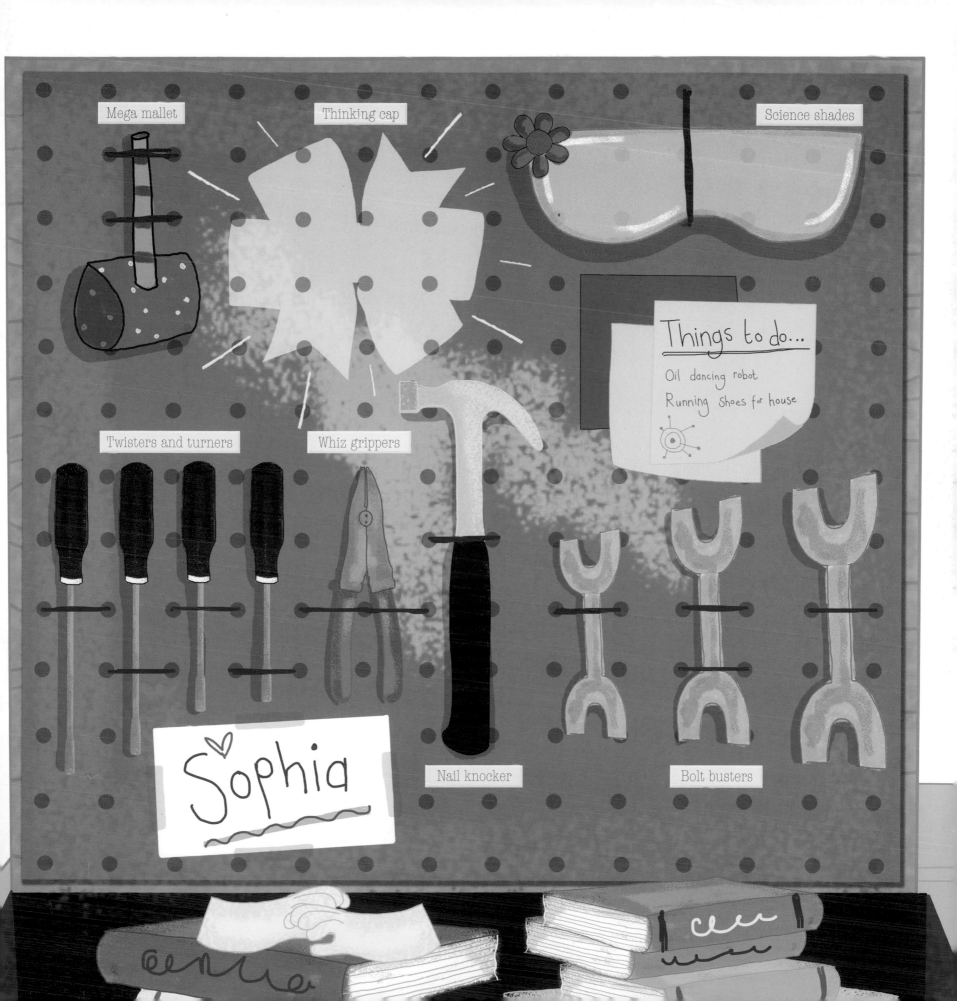

Her stomach, it **churned**.
Her spirits, they **sank**.

She thought,
with no *bow*,
that her mind would stay
BLANK!

Ldb

TOOLS

Meanwhile, the others
had worked at such a **pace**,
they were **already** bolting
INVENTIONS in place.

But her classmates' IDEAS
weren't working in **sync**,
and **no one** could work out
the **one MISSING** link.

"IT'S NO USE,"

cried *Sophia*,
as she **stormed** off to lunch ...
which was when, as it happened,
she had a great **hunch**.

She saw in the **shape**
of the **food** on her plate
how to blend their IDEAS
and make the bus **GREAT!**

She ran to the lab and, as **quick** as a FLASH,
showed all her friends
the **plan** made of
MASH!

"If we work alone, then we **won't** get this done.
But **TOGETHER**, we'll do it
and even have
FUN!"

The lab became noisy
with **hammers** and **drills**
as the LITTLE INVENTORS
used **ALL** of their skills.

At last they could see,
when they worked as a **team**,
they could make something
AWESOME...

BOW 1

"You've all **PASSED** the test,"
said their teacher with **glee.**

LOCAL TV | Breaking news : New school bus invented at Little Laboratory School •

"This **BUS** is so **cool,**
it's made
local TV!"

"You mixed your **inventions** to make every fixture. Kudos to *Sophia*, who **saw** the **big picture**."

While all of her CLASSMATES were watching the news, Sophia caught sight of her bow by their SHOES.

She picked it up quickly and said, her voice low,

"My IDEAS are **mine**, they don't come from this *bow!*"

But she tied it in place,
and then gave a **big grin**,
for the *bow* had let her know
her **ideas** were **within**.